A Lady's Doubt

The Everton Domestic Society
Book 4

A.S. Fenichel

ALL RIGHTS RESERVED

A LADY'S DOUBT Copyright © 2019 A.S. Fenichel

Second Edition © 2023 by A.S. Fenichel

All rights reserved.

No part of this book may be reproduced in any form or by any electronic or mechanical means, including information storage and retrieval systems, without written permission from the author, except for the use of brief quotations in a book review.

This book is a work of fiction and any resemblance to persons, living or dead, is purely coincidental. The characters are productions of the author's imagination. Locales are fictitious, and/or, are used fictitiously.

AI RESTRICTION: The author expressly prohibits any entity from using any part of this publication, including text and graphics, for purposes of training artificial intelligence (AI) technologies to generate text or graphics, including without limitation, technologies that are capable of generating works in the same style or genre as this publication.

The author reserves all rights to license uses of this work for generative AI training and development of machine learning language models.

Edited by Penny Barber

Cover design by LoveTheCover.com

A Lady's Doubt

Set on defying her greedy father, Roberta (Robbie) Fletcher refuses to marry an old codger and joins the Everton Domestic Society where she happily helps widows with correspondence and figures. When Miles Hallsmith proposes, she experiences a moment of elation. But, his admission he'd been sent by her father and his brother crush her heart. Instead of refusing him, she puts him to the task of finding out what their relatives have to gain from the match.

Miles had been smitten by Robbie from the moment he'd met her at a ball. As a third son with no means of supporting a wife, he'd had no right to court her. When the lady's father and his own despicable brother insist, he marry the object of his affection, he is torn between desire and suspicion.

Everton Ladies are notoriously brilliant and Robbie is not to be toyed with. Miles must prove his feelings are motivated by more than the lure of independence and money while thwarting his brother's disastrous plots. Bad blood and lingering doubts keep this couple apart. It will take honesty and cunning to bring them their heart's desire.

Acknowledgments

Special thanks to Penny Barber, my wonderful editor. She has been with me through ten books and made me a better writer with each one. Thanks to Gemma Brocato for helping me sort out this book to the fine story it is.

A Lady's Doubt is dedicated to all the wonderful readers who have embraced the world of The Everton Domestic Society with all their hearts. I can't thank you enough.

As always, for Dave, my heart, my soul, my love. Thank you.

Chapter One

Miles Hallsmith dreaded spending time with his brother Ford, but his monthly allowance depended on unwanted meetings with the Viscount of Thornbury. As the third son, Miles's options were limited. Regardless of his own wants, he was at his brother's mercy, so he traipsed through the Hallsmith townhouse.

His brother's voice boomed from the study, accompanied by a masculine voice Miles didn't recognize. Laughter filtered through the door.

Miles knocked.

Ford sat behind his large, bare desk with his feet perched at the edge. Since Miles took care of all Thornbury business, and for his trouble received enough money to survive, it was normal for Ford's desk to be devoid of papers. Ford's hands folded over his paunch accentuated how unhealthy he'd grown the past few years. His laughter stopped, though his grin remained. "Ah, Miles, good. Do you know Mr. Roberson Fletcher?"

Fletcher stood and bowed. His gray hair was long at the

collar and a weave of lines marked his face. It was hard to believe the charming young woman he'd met at a ball was this man's daughter.

Miles bowed then stepped forward and offered his hand. "We have not met. How do you do, Mr. Fletcher?"

"Very well. Very well, indeed." Fletcher and Ford shared a private smile.

Uneasiness settled in the pit of Miles's stomach whenever his brother was in a good humor. Aaron, the second Hallsmith son, was lucky. He'd been left a living and a piece of land in the north. Aaron wisely stayed out of Ford's purview.

Miles was not as lucky. He turned toward the desk. "You needed something, brother?

Dropping his feet to the floor, Ford sat forward. The sun shone in behind him, making it difficult to see his expression at the new angle.

It didn't matter. Whatever his brother wanted, Miles would likely do or find a way to conveniently forget.

Ford rested his arms on the desk. "It has all been arranged. You will go to the Everton Domestic Society today and propose marriage to Miss Roberta Fletcher."

A punch to the gut would have been less of a surprise. After a moment, his temper rose, requiring him to stifle a rant. "Why on earth would I do that?"

Standing, Ford was imposing to most. However, to Miles, it was all bluster and overused. "Because I command it!"

Miles sighed and sat in the chair next to the wide-eyed Mr. Fletcher. "I'm afraid you'll have to do better than that. I mean you nor your daughter offense, Mr. Fletcher. I have met the lady, and she is lovely. However, why this sudden urgency for us to marry?"

"You and your sister have been nothing but trouble to me

since you were born." Ford stormed around the desk and stared Miles down.

Feigning a yawn, Miles said, "You mean, my sister, the Viscountess of Devonrose? My sister, who shall be a countess one day. Is that the troublesome soul you speak of? A little respect, my lord."

"She may be titled, but she disobeyed me, and I shall never forgive her. You will do as I say or find yourself in the same condition."

Ford's belief that being disowned by him left anyone bereft was so comical it was sad. No one, including family members, mourned the loss of Ford's good opinion. He was an ass, and they all had come to accept that.

Putting his sister's happy loss aside, he focused on Ford. For Miles, Ford was his only source of income. "Besides your command, dear brother, why would I offer for Miss Fletcher, why would she accept, and when did she join the Everton Domestic Society?"

Ford's cheeks and neck turned bright red, and he pursed his lips. "My command is enough."

"I'm afraid not." Mile ignored Ford's insane rage and turned to Mr. Fletcher. "Sir, perhaps you can enlighten me on my three questions?"

Roberson Fletcher's graying brows drew together, and his knuckles whitened on the arms of the chair. He nodded toward Ford, who turned his back and pounded on the window frame. "Is he going to be all right?"

"Of course. This is quite natural for His Lordship." Miles forced a smile he hoped was reassuring enough to get him to the bottom of whatever was happening. "Now, when did your daughter join Everton's?"

Standing, Fletcher paced the rug. "A month ago, my daughter announced she would not marry and left home."

"Whom did you want her to marry?"

"The Earl of Granby."

"Lord, he must he sixty years old. I'm not surprised she refused." The idea of the fresh-faced Roberta Fletcher married to that crumpled old goat gnawed at Miles. She was full of life with wide eyes and bright smile, not to mention her curves. Better not to think on those too much.

"Fifty-nine, but that's not relevant. I demanded she marry, and she refused. I'll not be disobeyed again." Fletcher crossed his arms over his narrow chest. His gray hair stood out in all directions but up where he had no hair at all.

Trying his best to remain calm and resolve the matter, Miles realized Roberson Fletcher and Ford were of similar dispositions. He took several breaths before he continued. "Why would she accept me if she has made it clear she will not marry?"

Ford spun around. "You will convince her."

"That brings me back to my original question, gentlemen. Why would I ask Miss Fletcher to be my wife?" The memory of a pair of smiling blue eyes and blond hair slipped through his mind and sped his pulse.

Nostrils flaring like an old bull's, Ford narrowed his eyes. "Because, Mr. Fletcher has made it worth my while. He offers the property abutting Thornbury all the way to the river, plus Miss Fletcher has a substantial dowry."

Miles was not proud of the direction his thoughts spun. But there it was, the possibility of getting out from under his brother's thumb. "If I were to agree, and I'm not saying I want any part in this mess, I'd have some terms of my own that would need to be met."

A slow smile tugged at Mr. Fletcher's lips.

Ford sneered his derision. "What do you want? I already give you a living."

A Lady's Doubt

Standing, Miles met Ford's gaze directly. "A living which I earn by taking care of your entire estate and keeping you from falling into debtors' prison due to immense stupidity."

Unable to deny the claim, Ford bit his lip. "What do you want?"

"Should Miss Fletcher be willing to marry me, I will want her dowry to be transferred to us not you, Ford. I will also require a piece of land. The cottage and lands in Surrey should do nicely. I have always liked that property, and it is close to London. Further, you will hire a proper secretary to handle your affairs, as I will no longer be in need of your support."

"You ask too much." Spittle flew from Ford's mouth.

"Unless I'm mistaken, the property Mr. Fletcher offers is five or six times the size of the one I'm requesting and will bring an equal difference in income. I don't know what the dowry entails, but between the two, perhaps Miss Fletcher would be willing to marry a third son with little else to offer."

Fletcher put his hand out. "You have a deal, Mr. Hallsmith."

Grumbling Ford kicked a waste bin near the desk.

As he approached the front door of the Everton Domestic Society in Soho Square, Miles was certain all his good sense had gone out the window. The idea of escaping his brother's rule was too tempting.

Ford and Fletcher had suggested a dozen different ways to trick Roberta into marrying him. He'd considered just courting the very pretty, bright woman, but even then, there would be a lie between them.

After Mr. Fletcher had left, Ford made it clear that should Miles fail, things would not bode well for his future.

With a long sigh, Miles struck the knocker and waited.

The ancient butler, Gray, eased the door open like a crypt. "Mr. Hallsmith, how may I be of service?"

Before Miles's sister married the Viscount of Devonrose, she'd been an Everton lady. He had visited her at Everton House on several occasions and so was known to the staff. "I am sorry to arrive without an appointment, Gray. I wonder if Miss Roberta Fletcher is at home, and if she would be willing to see me?"

Bowing, Gray stepped back and allowed Miles to enter the foyer. The house was rich with dark woods and a sweeping staircase. At the bottom, a vase filled with spring flowers was the only feminine touch. A cherry odor of pipe tobacco wafted through the stately townhouse.

"Please wait in the parlor, sir. I'll see if Miss Fletcher is available for callers."

Miles followed Gray down the hallway to the side of the stairs and into a very small parlor that faced the back garden. Spring flowers spilled out over the veranda, and the open window allowed their heady fragrance within.

At a snail's pace, Gray ambled back down the hallway. The sun coming through a window putting him in silhouette.

Even with the time avoiding his task, and the ride over in his carriage, Miles had no idea what he was going to say. He stared out the window at the stunning garden, enjoying the wildness allowed to take over.

"Mr. Hallsmith?"

As lovely as the first time he'd seen her at a ball with Sylvia Dowder as her Everton Lady escort, Roberta Fletcher smile, wide eyes and blushing cheeks warming him to his toes. His pulse raced as he took in her curves, which a full skirt of white muslin couldn't hide.

A Lady's Doubt

He bowed. "Miss Fletcher. It is a pleasure to see you again."

He really meant it, but as soon as she learned why he'd come, she would never believe him. A knot formed in his chest.

Making a pretty curtsy, she cast her gaze down. "It is nice to see you too, though I'm at a loss for why you have come."

"Can we sit for a few minutes?" He waited until she had crossed the threshold and sat on the divan before he sat across from her in a very uncomfortable chair with brown and white cushions and spindly legs.

"Shall I call for some tea?" She folded her hands in her lap, moved them apart then together again. Finally, she put one on either side of her legs.

"I don't require tea at this time. I've come at the behest of my brother and your father, I'm afraid."

Her sweet smile fell. "Hell in a handcart, and I liked you very much until now. Why must everything be ruined?"

Shocked and amused by her colorful language, he held his chuckle back. "Is it quite certain you cannot like me?"

Shaking her head, she sighed. "My father has little concern for my happiness and has probably sent you to marry me or with some other nefarious plan. I don't know your brother, but have not heard good things."

Unable to argue he nodded. Lying to her bothered him more than her tossing him from the house, which of course, she would do in just a few moments. "My brother, the Viscount of Thornbury, commanded me to marry you. He and your father have made a financial arrangement."

Sorrow filled her eyes, when he was expecting rage. A single tear slid down her pale cheek.

Miles inched around the low mahogany table and sat next to her. "I did not mean to cause you pain, Miss Fletcher."

With watery eyes, she looked up at him. "What did you want then?"

"My brother suggested I fill you with falsehoods and woo you with pretty sonnets. He believes all women respond to lies and deceit. I could not bear it, so I thought to try the truth."

"What is the truth?" She wiped away her tears. "You say you were commanded to marry me, and my father has an arrangement with your brother. Why would that send you running here in all this state? We danced one time, and I saw nothing of you afterward. You did not seek me out or call. Why on earth would you want to marry me now?"

He'd made a complete muddle of this. "You're right. I did nothing after a lovely dance with a beautiful woman. You were very young, and I had nothing to offer you. I am a third son who depends on the sporadic kindness of a villainous brother for my own support. How was I to show that in any kind of good light? Your father would have tossed me from the house, and rightfully so."

She stared, but one side of those ruby lips tipped up in spite of her silence.

"I apologize for my awkwardness, Miss Fletcher. None of that is your fault or your concern. I only wanted to convey that had my circumstances been more favorable, I would have continued our acquaintance."

"Is that true?" Roberta's sweet blush returned, disappearing below the neckline of her day dress.

"It is, however, irrelevant. I am here today to ask for your hand, as I believe it will be advantageous to both of us." Lord, he sounded like an ass.

Ladies' laughter filtered in through the open door, and the reverberation of sensible shoes on wooden stairs followed.

Roberta sat motionless until silence returned. "I've been quite happy here this last month. I have a talent for writing and have been helping Lady Dramthorn with her correspondence. I'm also good with numbers and have helped several widows understand their accounts. It is safe here at the Everton Domestic Society. I earn my own money and can come and go as I please. What is it you are offering, or should I say, what is it your brother is offering?"

Suddenly, his coming was the most selfish act he'd ever committed. "I suppose very little. I should have followed my first instinct and turned my brother down. Of course, he probably would have disowned me, and I would have to go and live with one of my other siblings."

He stood his gut aching with regret. He'd allowed Ford to make him abhorrent to himself, and worse, to a young woman he sincerely liked. "Forgive me. I'll not take any more of your time."

As he passed between her and the table, she clasped his hand. "I have been unkind, and I am sorry. My father brings out the worst in me, and I can see you have similar problems with your brother."

Soft warmth, like arriving at his parents' country home after a long absence, filled him. It had been many years since his father passed, since anywhere had felt like home. Yet her ungloved hand in his...

He shook off the notion. "You are kind to take any of the blame. I am solely at fault for this awkwardness."

Staring at their clasped hands, she looked as bewildered as he felt. "You came and did not follow the edicts of those other men. What were you promised to marry me, if I might ask?"

Unable to tell her while touching her, he eased his hand away and took a few steps toward the open doorway. The room was too small to create any real distance, but being so close, he struggled to breathe. "A very fine piece of income property with a lovely cottage in Surrey and your dowry."

"Your brother was keen on giving you the property?"

Lord, she was clever. "No. I had to refuse first. He is gaining a very large parcel from your father, which abuts the Thornbury country estate."

She nodded. "And what is my father gaining?"

"I assumed you in a secure marriage."

Shaking her head, she rolled her eyes. "No. There must be something more, sir. My father's concern for my wellbeing is slight at best. He planned to marry me off to a feeble old man because the marriage agreement came with a large sum of money and a parcel of land upon the earl's death. My father thought to gain those properties. He went so far as to forbid me to give the earl a son and ruin his plans."

Ford and Roberson made quite a pair. The idea of her producing children with the Earl of Granby set his stomach in a roil. "I'm sorry your father is not more concerned with your feelings, Miss Fletcher. However, I can't fathom what he might gain monetarily from our union."

A line formed between her eyes, and her frown deepened. "Yet there is something we don't know. I can assure you of that."

If he could have thought of anything that would make her smile as she had in the ballroom the first time they'd met, he would have done it. He longed for her slightly wicked and blushing disposition, yet all he gave her was dismay.

Saving him from having to say anything, she continued, "I thank you for your proposal, but I cannot accept at this time."

His pulse pounded harder. It was not the outright refusal he'd expected. He should have been happy to have her reject him outright. Then he could have gone back to his brother, and this entire mess would be forgotten in a week's time. Hopeful, he couldn't resist knowing more. "Under what conditions might your wishes change?"

As she swallowed, he followed the bob of her throat and longed to place his lips there. Miles shook aside the unwelcome bout of desire.

"I'm really not sure, Mr. Hallsmith. You are clearly a nice man. I have not had the opportunity to meet your sister, but she was an Everton Lady and is spoken of very highly here. I liked you quite a lot on our first meeting, but as you say, my father would not have approved the match."

Stepping closer, he breathed in her warm floral essence. It took him several moments to regain his composure. "I am not keen on doing anything my brother has devised, Miss Fletcher, but you are lovely, and I find myself unable to let go of the notion. There must be something said for that."

Fool that he was, her chuckle sent a jolt of delight through him.

"You might find out what Father is gaining. Perhaps that information will sway your decision." The rooms small size, put her directly in front of him when she stood.

Miles had no desire to back away. In fact, he longed to bring her closer. Propriety and the open door rooted him in place. "Or you might have a change of heart."

A hint of a smile lit her dark blue eyes. "I cannot say, sir."

Unable to breathe, he forced himself to step away. "I will investigate the situation. My brother is terrible at hiding information, as he feels all should abide his rule without question. It rarely works out for him. Shall I call again, when I know more?"

"I think you visiting Everton House again would cause talk I can ill afford."

His hopes fell.

"I will be at the Rushmore ball. If you do find anything of note, you might impart that knowledge there."

Heart beating out of his chest, he bowed. "And if I know nothing, but would like to dance with you anyway?"

There was the delectable blush he remembered. "I know of nothing which would keep us from enjoying a dance, sir."

"Until then." He bowed and rushed from Everton House before he made a complete fool of himself.

Chapter Two

Roberta must have lost her mind. Sitting in the very parlor where he had visited, she fretted over the meeting. She would have been better served by tossing Miles Hallsmith from the house and never seeing him again. He was in league with her father, and nothing good had ever come from that man. In fact, Father had ruined the lovely memory she'd kept of dancing with Miles so long ago. It had been the one bright spot in her seasons in town.

She had spent her first season with two Everton ladies, and both had been wonderful, if unsuccessful in getting her married off. The Everton Domestic Society had been a good choice for her. Despite her being much younger than most women who choose career over marriage, she was confident it was the best place for her.

"Am I disturbing you, Robbie?" Ann Wittman stepped inside the small parlor. Ann had been kind and helpful since Roberta had met her, and they had gotten on well.

"Not at all. I've been wool gathering."

"Oh?" Ann sat next to her on the divan. "Is there something troubling you?"

"I'm certain you've heard about my visitor." While Everton ladies were not given to gossip, it was impossible to hide anything as grand as a gentleman calling in the middle of the day.

"Yes, I heard Mr. Hallsmith came to see you. Did he say something to upset you?" Her gray eyes softened, and she patted Roberta's hand.

Roberta was unable to hold back a long sigh. "He asked me to marry him. At least, I think he did. It's all a mess."

Eyes wide, Ann got up, closed the door and returned to the divan. "Do you wish to marry Mr. Hallsmith?"

"I might have a year ago, but now I'm not sure. The circumstances are distressing." Without really meaning to, Roberta told Ann everything that had transpired between herself and Miles. At the end of her story, she had to hold back tears. Whether she was upset by her father's involvement or her own actions, she couldn't say.

Ann sat silently for several beats before smiling. "You are not indifferent to him if your passionate telling is any indication."

"I suppose not." Indifferent was one thing she certainly wasn't. During her first season, the way he looked at her had shot her heart into a staccato beat, and that look had not changed.

A single curl of blond hair had come loose from Ann's severe bun. She tucked it back in with precision. "He is a very good man. His sister Phoebe adores him and told us nothing but good things about him when she worked here."

"Sylvia Dowder also spoke highly of him." Him being so good made Roberta feel even worse. If he were a villain, she

A Lady's Doubt

could brush him aside as another of her father's plots. His good character made that ever so much harder.

"It seems to me, he could easily have lied and found his way into your heart. You liked him in the ballroom, and he must have liked you too. He came to you and divulged the entire story, knowing it would cost him to do so."

"Cost him? What do you mean?" Running the scene back through her mind, she couldn't remember any mention of consequences beyond not getting her money or his brother's property.

Ann leaned closer. "If he succeeds, he will be independent for the first time in his life. He's a third son. This is his only means of getting out from under his brother's thumb. However, if he fails, don't you think it's possible his brother will cut him loose? I've not heard many good things about Ford Hallsmith. In order to induce Miles into taking such an action, the threat must have been very grave."

Slumping against the arm of the divan, she thumped her head on the wood frame. "I'm a selfish cow. It never occurred to me that his circumstances might be worse than my own."

Patting her hand, Ann smiled. "I expect you have a lot on your mind, and it would have occurred to you at some point."

"Perhaps." It had been foolish to believe she had left feeling dreadful behind when she escaped her father's rule. That man had a way of spoiling everything.

"Have you agreed to see Mr. Hallsmith again?"

Perhaps she could make amends for her behavior. A glimmer of hope made all the rest slip away. "We are to meet at the Rushmore ball. I promised Mother I would attend. She will badger me to death, but I couldn't say no."

Ann rose and pulled the cord to call for tea. "Perhaps you will find nothing nefarious afoot, and all will be well."

Roberta wished she could believe it, but even with her

limited experience things rarely turned out for the good when her father was involved.

Mother had picked Roberta up, and for the entire forty-minute ride to the Rushmore ball, had done nothing but criticize. "I should never have allowed you to meet with Mr. Hallsmith at that Everton House. Your father had no right to arrange such a thing without consulting me. You likely chased him off without giving me an opportunity to tell him about all your attributes."

It did little good to wish Mother believed half of the things she would tell suitors about her only daughter. Spewing lies about how accomplished Roberta was came second nature to Lenora. "Mother, Mr. Hallsmith said he would be here, and I'm sure he will not disappoint you."

"I'm very vexed with your father for arranging a husband for you without consulting me." She hid a satisfied smile behind her ruby fan. Lenora Fletcher didn't look the least bit put out. In fact, she might burst with unbridled elation at any moment.

"We'll see."

A crush overfilled the small rooms of the Rushmore townhouse. Blocking the passage, several young men were having a dispute. Roberta leaned against the wall and faced her mother. "Why is Father so keen on me marrying? After all, I'm no longer a burden to either of you."

Mother blinked several times, her expression changing from confusion, to blank stare, and then annoyance. "Your father wants you to be happy and settled. Why are you always looking for trouble, Roberta? This is not how I raised you. And for heaven's sake, stand up straight." Mother pushed through the throng, scolding the young men for their rudeness as she went.

Put in their proper place, the men stared after Mother, looking contrite.

Keeping her head down, Roberta took advantage of her mother's tirade and followed her into the ballroom.

Avoiding eye contact with anyone, she scurried to the other side of the room, where she found a quiet corner away from her mother and safe from gossip. The music started, and couples got ready for the minuet.

Wishing she could go back to her first season and enjoy the ball would not rewrite reality. Just as any young woman does, she'd come out with high hopes of falling in love. When her mother hired the Everton Domestic Society to help her be more at ease with gentlemen who might take interest, she'd embraced the notion. She tended to say whatever was on her mind, and that was not always popular with potential suitors.

She should have known Father had other plans. It had always been about gaining money and power. If only she could determine whether Miles was part of the problem or a possible solution.

"Gathering wool in the corner is no way to spend a ball, Robbie." Sylvia Braighton, the new Countess of Grafton, smiled and made a curtsy.

Her own curtsy was quick as Roberta filled with renewed energy. "I'm so happy to see you. Relieved really. I could use a friend right now, Sylvie."

Concern etched a line between Sylvia's brows. She stepped close and lowered her voice. "Whatever is wrong, Robbie? Are you feeling well?"

"I'm fine. Well, not really. I mean to say my health is fine. Father has been up to his tricks again."

"Not another old man, I hope." Sylvia crossed her arms and frowned.

A memory of Miles's kind eyes and inviting smile warmed Roberta's cheeks.

"Are you blushing? What is going on?" Sylvia whispered.

"The other day Miles Hallsmith came to call. He was sent by my father and his brother to propose marriage." A butterfly war erupted in Roberta's stomach.

Sylvia blinked owlishly. "Miles, really? He's a very nice man, Robbie. You could do far worse."

"I know, but Father—I don't trust any of it. I doubt that any of these men are telling me the truth as they all tend to be after their own gains." She didn't like the shaky tone of her own voice, and even more disturbing, she couldn't decide if her unease was due to Father's manipulations or her own attraction to Miles.

Taking Roberta's hand and giving it a squeeze, Sylvia plastered a pleasant expression on her face. "Gather your wits; he is coming over."

"Who is?" Roberta turned as Miles strode to a stop directly in front of her. Tall and graceful with that dark red hair and those piercing blue eyes, he took her breath. She couldn't look away.

He bowed. "Ladies. It is lovely to see you. Lady Grafton, I didn't know you and Tony would be attending."

Wicked smile firmly in place, Sylvia said, "We return to the country next week, but Tony's mother wished to attend, as she and Lady Rushmore have become friends. In fact, I must find her. If you two will excuse me? Robbie, do come for tea this week."

Sylvia sauntered away grinning like a cat with a bowl of cream. It was hard to be upset with her, though. "She might try to be a bit less obvious."

A Lady's Doubt

His laugh rumbled right through Robbie and settled pleasantly low in her belly. Smiling through those lovely eyes, he asked, "Do you always say what you're thinking, Miss Fletcher?"

"A failing of mine, sir. I'm sure to offend you in short order."

His unwavering gaze made it hard to think. "I find it refreshing. At least I know what you think, rather than having to guess."

"Most people have little care about what I'm thinking and would prefer I keep it to myself."

Leaning in so only she could hear him, he filled her senses with his warm woodsy scent. "I am not most people, Robbie. Oh, I do like this name for you."

It took her several beats to recover from his familiarity and proximity. "It is only used by my particular friends, Mr. Hallsmith. You and I are not yet beyond formality. Or perhaps you bring news you believe will change that?"

"Of course, you're right. Forgive me." He shifted and clasped his hands behind his back. "I'm hesitant to discuss such things in the crowded ballroom."

Mother was pushing her way around the ballroom while eating some kind of pudding.

Cringing internally, Roberta sighed. "We might meet in the garden. Lady Rushmore usually keeps the veranda well lit. For now, I must apologize."

Confusion colored his expression. "Whatever for?"

"Mr. Hallsmith," Lenora gushed. "I'm so pleased to see you have found my dear Roberta. As you can see, she is in good health. Her teeth are excellent. She plays the pianoforte quite well. Last year she painted the most stunning tea set. You cannot imagine a better person with both writing and figuring."

Mortification grew within Roberta. Stomach churning until

she thought she might become ill, she took three steps back, partially hiding herself beside the hearth. The fact was Mother meant well. It was just that she had few morals about what she was willing to say to marry Roberta off and little tact in the delivery of the information.

Sadly, Roberta saw shades of her mother in her own desire to speak up when she should keep quiet. She searched the room for an escape.

"Madam, you are too kind to deliver all of this indisputable information to one so humble as I. However, I can assure you, my captivation with Miss Fletcher is well solidified." Miles bowed but shifted his amusement-filled gaze to Roberta. "I was hoping to ask her for the next dance, if that is acceptable to you both?"

Mother opened and closed her mouth like a large fish deprived of water. When she recovered, her grin was almost as embarrassing. "I'm positive Roberta would delight in a dance."

Unable and unwilling to ignore his attempt at rescue, Roberta accepted his arm. "She'll be talking of nothing else for a week."

He stopped but didn't extend his arms for the waltz. "If dancing with me is abhorrent to you, Miss Fletcher, you are not required to follow through."

Frustration warred with how much she liked him. "Forgive me, sir. Of course, I want to dance with you. I'm just embarrassed by my mother, which makes me feel guilty. My decision to become an Everton Lady, while necessary, was still selfish. I have not fully recovered."

Offering his open arms, he waited until she stepped into them. As the music began, Miles whirled them around the dance floor. "Some acts of selfishness are required for survival."

"You are too kind." Despite the warmth of his arms and his soft voice meant only for her, she chilled at the sight of her mother watching and chattering with Lady Pemberhamble, the most notorious gossip in all of London.

Miles turned them through the throng of dancers until they were obscured from Mother's view. "Tell me, Miss Fletcher, what exactly did you paint on the tea set?"

The mood instantly lightened. "I believe Mother may have exaggerated."

One side of his full mouth lifted. "In what way?"

"I did paint a tea set, but it was when I was twelve, and it is so hideous it has been hidden in the attic these eight years. My playing of the pianoforte is abominable, and my teeth are only tolerable." A giggle escaped, but when he smiled, all she could do was imagine how it would be to kiss those lips.

Missing a step, he faltered. "What were you just thinking?"

"I'd rather not say." But she couldn't keep her gaze away from his mouth.

His arms tightened. "I see." Easing close to her ear, he whispered, "I would like very much to kiss you, too."

Roberta's heart stopped, even as they whirled around the floor. "I am quite good with correspondence and figures."

Once she'd blurted it out, she wanted to run away. But wanting him to find something of value about her won, and she had said it.

When the music ended, Miles released her and bowed. "You need not sell yourself to me, Robbie. I did not exaggerate when I told your good mother that you captivate me."

"Are you certain it is not my dowry and a fine piece of property that you are attracted by?" Roberta cupped her hand over her mouth. Her fears had blurted forth before she could stop them.

His sigh said enough to let her know he would walk away and never speak to her again. "I've promised to partner Miss

Rushmore for the next. Would you be so kind as to meet me on the veranda after that?"

"I...I'll do my best to get away." It was rare that Roberta didn't know what to say. Her response was met with a nod, and she rushed to find a place to hide and regain her wits.

Thankful the crowd allowed her to avoid her mother, Roberta slipped into a small niche near the back of the room. Long deep breaths gave her some stability.

Sylvia appeared, startling her. "What's wrong? Did Miles say something to upset you? When I saw you run to this alcove, I imagined the worst."

Tears welled behind her eyes. "He was a perfect gentleman."

"Then why are you crying?" Sylvia offered a handkerchief from her reticule.

Dabbing her eyes, Roberta swallowed the rest of her tears. "I insulted him. I don't know why I did it, but suddenly I thought of my father and his brother conspiring, and my worst thoughts popped out of my mouth."

"Oh, dear." Sylvia pulled her into a hug. "Well, he may as well get used to it."

Pushing away, Roberta asked, "What does that mean."

Her gaze direct, Sylvia said, "It means that you have a habit of speaking before you think, and if Miles wants to marry you, he'll have to get used to it."

All the air went out of Roberta. "He will never wish to marry a viper."

With an amused grin, Sylvia patted her cheek. "You are not a viper, Robbie. You are sweet and kind. No one is a better friend than you. It is one bad habit amongst an abundance of wonderful attributes."

"Thank you for that." She'd always lashed out when afraid. At twenty years old, she should be better than that.

A Lady's Doubt

"Did he seem very put out?"

"He frowned but asked me to meet him on the veranda after this dance."

"I suggest you pull yourself together and see what he has to say."

Roberta closed her eyes and cleared her mind of all the terrible things her father had arranged in the last year. She let each offense slip through her mind before she let them go. "I'm feeling much better. Thank you for worrying about me, Sylvie. I don't know what I would do without your friendship and Ann's."

"We Everton Ladies always stick together. You can be sure of my loyalty, my dear Robbie. There are the families we are born to, and then the families we collect as we grow and learn. You are a good friend, and I am lucky to have you in my life."

"Thank you." She fought back a bout of happy tears.

"I have to go. Anthony is waving. I think he wants to leave. He can't stand these crowds, and his mother has made her appearance for her friend. Come to Collington House tomorrow for tea and tell me all about this meeting with Miles. Maybe I can help you work through all the details and help decide the best thing for you." Sylvia kissed her cheek.

"I'll see you tomorrow."

With a smile, Sylvia strode like a queen across the ballroom, her emerald gown flowing around her like sea waves.

Chapter Three

After his compulsory dance with the overly excitable Miss Rushmore, Miles went out to the veranda to meet Robbie. Several levels with stone balusters and grand staircases gave guests a fine view of the lush gardens. Torches and a full moon lit the garden enough to view several couples and groups strolling the paths.

Keeping to the shadow of the house, he remained in a corner, watching and waiting. If she were sensible, she'd stay away from a clandestine meeting with a man. Miles sent up a small prayer that Robbie wasn't sensible.

Anthony Braighton, the Earl of Grafton, stepped out of the ballroom and scanned the veranda. He had a slight limp from a horrific accident a year prior. Someone not looking for the hitch in his step was unlikely to even notice.

"Who are you looking for, Tony?" Miles stepped out of the shadows.

A broad smile spread across Tony's face. "Sylvia just told me you were here. I wanted to see for myself before we went home as I hardly believed it."

A Lady's Doubt

Avoiding the ballroom had become a bad habit. Since Miles had no fortune, he was not much missed by those mothers searching for husbands for their daughters. Still, he was the son of a viscount and had some value. "Rushmore was a good friend to my father, and he asked me to come and dance with his daughter."

Tony cocked his head and raised an eyebrow. "And?"

"And nothing." Miles kept one eye on the door in case Robbie was fool enough to meet him.

Crossing his arms over his chest, Tony flattened his lips. "You are a good poker player, but that does not mean you are a good liar. What are you up to?"

"Coming from the worst liar and poker player in all of England, I must be very obvious." A blonde stepped out, catching Miles's eye, but his heart deflated immediately. She was tall and slim, not voluptuous like his Robbie. When had he started thinking of her as his? He shook off the notion.

"Who are you looking for?"

"No one."

"If you don't tell me, I'll send my wife out here to drag it out of you." Tony laughed.

Since Robbie and Sylvia were friends, it was possible Tony's wife already knew his secret. "I'm to meet Miss Roberta Fletcher. However, the lady seems to have come to her senses and decided not to show herself."

From interest to intrigue, a world of thoughts crossed Tony's face. Finally, he said, "I imagine there is a story, and when you need a friend's ear, I shall be at your disposal. I wanted to say hello and goodbye. We are leaving. I only came because my mother wished it, and now, I want to take my wife home for the evening. I hope Miss Fletcher shows herself."

With a bow, Tony left, and Miles was grateful for his understanding.

Long past the end of the dance, when it seemed clear Robbie would not come, she stepped out on the veranda. Her pale blue gown caught the breeze, showing off her stunning figure as the silk pressed against her flesh. Miles didn't know if he'd ever been jealous of fabric before, but he wanted to touch her just as intimately.

Shaking himself, he said, "Miss Fletcher?"

She turned, her blue eyes wide and mouth agape. "Hello."

"You seem surprised." He stepped back, hoping she'd move away from the ballroom lights.

Stepping closer, she lowered her voice. "I'm late."

Pain lanced his chest. "And you hoped I would have gone already."

Closer still, she touched his arm. Then realizing her mistake, snatched her hand away. "Please don't be offended, Mr. Hallsmith. You seem like a very nice man. I—my father and I have many differences of opinion where my future is concerned."

Her long sigh urged him to take her in his arms and give her comfort, but of course, that was not possible. "I understand and have had similar issues with my brother. Will you walk with me in the garden, or is that asking too much?"

"I think that will be fine." Clutching her hands in front of her, she fell in step beside him. "Have you learned anything about this plan of our relations?"

Probably unaware that when she gripped her hands, it pushed her full breasts to the brink of her gown, she couldn't know the distraction and discomfort she caused him. "Only that you are probably correct. My brother is quite close-mouthed about whatever the private arrangement is with Mr. Fletcher. This is not a normal state for Ford. Usually, he is keen on telling everyone how clever he is."

Her giggle sent a wave of joy through him. "And is he clever?"

"Never." Miles could watch her smile and listen to her laugh all night long.

"I don't believe my mother knows anything about the situation. She tends to stick to what is obvious and not dig too deeply into Father's affairs. Sadly, this is probably wise if she wishes to be content in their marriage."

Stopping, he faced her. "What do you want, Robbie? I know I should call you Miss and act as if your feelings in this matter count for nothing. I should convince you to marry me so that I can get away from Ford once and for all. However, I do not want a wife who tolerates, or worse, hates me."

Those dark blue eyes were wide and filled with so much emotion. He didn't know if she would laugh, cry, or rage at him. Finally, she whispered, "I want love, Miles. I want a grand passion that cannot be compared. If I can't marry for such a love, then I prefer to not marry at all."

Caught between adoration and despair, Miles didn't know what to say. Could such a love actually exist? Robbie obviously believed it could, and she did so with such fervor he almost believed it too. Yet, she hadn't said she loved him, and he didn't know if he was even capable of such emotion. "I think that admirable."

"And impractical," she added with a chuckle.

"Perhaps, but that does not make such a thing impossible." Suddenly, he longed to believe it could happen, and not only that. He wished for it to happen for her. Miles wanted Robbie to have her magnificent love.

"May I ask you something, Miles?" She'd become tentative and uncomfortable compared to the vibrant woman he'd met at Everton House and on the dance floor.

"Anything." Once again, they walked the lighted path

through the garden.

"What will happen to you if you fail in convincing me to marry you?"

A lie would be easier on her, and the truth, perhaps, would bind her to him. Either choice was poor. "I wish you would not ask me that."

"You said I might ask anything. Are you changing your mind? Am I only permitted to ask questions you want to answer?" There was the fire that intrigued him.

He offered her a seat on a stone bench near a bubbling fountain filled with cherub statues in various postures of play. "If I reply, you must promise what I tell you will have no bearing on your decision."

"How can I make such a promise?" She spread her arms then let them drop.

Sitting, he took one hand from her lap and kissed her knuckles. Her soft skin warmed every inch of him and reminded him how much he'd liked her long before Ford had stepped in and complicated things. "Then will you promise you will not say yes based on what I tell you?"

Robbie stared at their joined hands. "I promise."

He withdrew his hand. A deep emptiness settled inside him. "Ford has made it clear that he will disown me should I fail. There is no allowance partitioned for me, the third son. My brother Adam is lucky as he will receive a sum from the estate regardless of Ford's whims. I keep his books, and he pays me for that service."

"Then you will be destitute if I don't marry you?" Tears shone in her eyes.

He thumbed away one that rolled down her sweet cheek. "I will survive. I have put away a decent sum and have many friends with whom I can find employment."

Confusion filled her gaze. "I don't know what to do. On the

A Lady's Doubt

one hand, I do like you, and on the other, my father sullies everything."

Her confession made him feel both good and terrible. She wanted that grand passion, and he wanted it for her. Liking him was not her dream. Yet, it was not a total dismissal either. "It is too soon to decide such a thing. May I have permission to walk with you in the park tomorrow?"

"It must be a very fine piece of land for you to continue this ridiculous courtship." Her long sigh was heartbreaking.

As the dinner hour neared, the garden had grown very quiet. Miles ran his knuckles along her jaw to her cheek. "It is a gift to spend time with you, Robbie. I wish my brother had not made it so you would find that difficult to believe, but regardless, it is the truth."

"Are you going to kiss me now?" Her voice trembled.

"I would like to more than I can say, but only if you wish it too." He held his breath.

"I have never kissed anyone." Her cheeks warmed to his touch.

It should not have been possible to be swamped by so much happiness. It was only a kiss. She was not his lover. Yet, there it was, this fully bloomed desire pulsing inside him. And not just for lust, though that was there as well. He needed her to want him as well. "Then the decision should be yours and yours alone, my sweet."

She leaned in until her lips touched his.

Innocent as it was, the perfection of the kiss ignited Miles's heart. He drew her bottom lip between his and on her gasp, did the same with her shapely top lip.

She relaxed against his him and followed his lead, tasting him as if he were some rare delicacy.

When he slid his tongue between those supple lips, she met his touch. The world stopped, leaving only the two of them in the garden with the bubbling of the fountain and Robbie's sighs.

Her disappointed groan as he forced himself away would ring in his soul for an eternity. "I think, it is safe to say"—he gulped down an unsteady breath—"there is some attraction between us."

Hand still caressing her cheek, she was like fine silk on his fingertips. "Then this is not what all kisses are like?"

"I don't know about all kisses, but kissing you was by far the most remarkable moment of my life, Robbie."

"What if you're just saying that for my dowry and a piece of property?"

Dropping his hand away left him wanting, but there was no help for it. "We have a problem. Because of the agreement between my brother and your father, you doubt me. I don't blame you, since you don't know me. However, if I don't force Ford to give me the property, I will not have the means to support a wife and family."

Robbie stood and stepped toward the fountain. "I see your point. I, on the other hand, am perfectly settled at the Everton Domestic Society and can continue to help people with their correspondence until one day I'm old enough to become a chaperone at Everton's. I can have a perfectly adequate life."

Leaning in, he touched the delicate curls resting on her neck. "I might have been content too, before that kiss. Now I'll always long for another."

She turned, bringing her chest against his, then nearly toppled backward to get away.

Saving her from the fountain, Miles pulled her into his arms. Wide-eyed, she stared up at him with total trust. He kissed her forehead and eased away. "Walk with me in the park tomorrow. I'll ask at White's tonight and see if I can find out what Ford and your father are up to."

Her throat bobbed, and she took several steps away from him. "You didn't mention the dowry. You would also gain my dowry. It's quite a lot of money."

"I thought we might put that away for our children so their decisions might be made without the worry of finances when the time came."

"You would do that?"

"I know all too well the lot of a less valued child. I hope that if I am ever blessed with children, they will all feel equal in both finances and parental love." He didn't blame his father. The entailment did not include a third son. His parents loved him and had made sure he was indispensable to the estate. However, when his father died, Ford made it just as clear he would hire a secretary and be rid of Miles, if ever he felt the whim.

She sat on the bench, and her gown fluffed around her. "Wouldn't it have been nice to just be loved by my parents and not used as a bargaining chip? I will give it some thought, Miles. If you like, you may escort me to Collington House for tea tomorrow."

"It would be my pleasure." Once he left her at the veranda, it was wise to leave the Rushmore ball. No need to put her mother into a tizzy about where they had been or that they'd been in the garden alone. Instead, he slipped out the side gate and went to White's.

The gentleman's club was nearly as crowded as the ball had been. Men were all buzzing about the upcoming votes in the House of Lords. Miles stayed out of politics, though he kept abreast of what was happening.

In a few short weeks, the vote to abolish the slave trade was likely to pass. It wasn't what is should be, but it was a step in the right direction toward freedom for all. Miles prayed it would pass. Even Ford was on the side of right with this particular vote. It was highly debated in every room at Whites.

Unwilling to join the fray, Miles stalked the stately rooms looking for someone who might know Roberson Fletcher well enough to give some insight into what Ford had promised.

As Miles passed the card room, Fletcher's familiar voice boomed down the hall. "I have no worries about my assets, Lester. You shall see there is nothing to fear from the House of Lords."

Fletcher spoke as if he had a say in such things. He might be a rich gentleman, but he was not titled and did not carry a vote. Perhaps it was time to look into what kind of investments Robbie's father had.

It was ungentlemanly, but Miles tarried in the hall longer than was necessary.

"How can you be sure of that, Fletcher. The current atmosphere points to stopping slave trading to the new world," Lester said. His voice laced with nervous hesitation.

"Not to worry. Your investment is safe."

"Miles, what are you doing?" Thomas Wheel slinked down the hall and spoke in a whisper. Worry etched lines around his mouth.

"Behaving beneath myself, but for a good cause." He waved his friend into another room. Sitting, he rubbed his forehead. "What would Roberson Fletcher have to gain from the slave trade continuing?"

Thomas ordered two brandies and waited for the footman to step out of the room before he answered. "Fletcher has a great deal of investments in the Caribbean. Abolition would be inconvenient for him."

A knot curled in Miles's gut. "I have a very bad feeling."

"Something I can help with?" Thomas had been his friend since Eton. He was a good man who had a lot of connections. It was no surprise he knew what kind of business Fletcher was involved with.

"I have a feeling my brother has sold his vote, and he's using me to make the arrangement appear above board."

The brandy arrived, and again, Thomas waited for the server to step out. "How is he doing that?"

"By offering me exactly what I want." Miles explained the entire mess to Thomas. When he spoke of Robbie, his heart ached with regret.

"Your tone tells me Miss Fletcher is also part of what you want. The law will pass. One vote will make little difference. Why not get out from under Ford and live happily ever after with the lovely Miss Fletcher?" Thomas sipped his drink.

"My guess is Ford's is not the only vote Fletcher has bought, but that is not as much of an issue as my brother's lack of morals. When she hears of this, she'll not want anything to do with my family." The pain in his chest tightened. He'd not even wanted to marry a few days ago, but losing Robbie hurt more than anything he'd ever endured.

"Forgive me, Miles, but I doubt anyone would be surprised by your brother's lack of concern for the plight of others. Nor Fletcher's for that matter. I suggest you discuss it with the lady and see what she thinks. I don't know her well, but having met her on two occasions, I was struck by how bright she is. If you really like her, give her the facts.

"And if she sends me packing?"

A grin spread across Thomas's face. "Then you make an ass of yourself until you convince her she can't live without you."

Unable to help laughing, Miles attempted a stern look. "I don't even know if the lady returns my feelings."

Thomas leaned forward. "And what are your feelings?"

He downed his brandy. "Complicated."

Thomas chuckled as he called for another round.

Chapter Four

Robbie forced herself to stop biting her nails. It was a terrible habit she'd all but cured herself of unless under great stress. Riding in Miles's carriage on the way to tea with Sylvia shouldn't make her nervous. It was ridiculous. Even more preposterous was her fear of hearing whatever he might have learned about her father.

"Do I make you uncomfortable, Robbie?" In the open carriage, they were exposed to all of London. Miles rode backward for her sake, but his warm smile was too intimate after the kiss in the garden.

He might have snatched part of her soul in that kiss, but it was no reason to act like a ninny. "No. Should you be calling me by such a familiar name, Mr. Hallsmith?"

"Yes. I believe I should. I further believe you should call me Miles as I adore the sound of it from your lips."

"Goodness, are you flirting with me?" Heart pounding, she should have either admonished him or acted the shy debutante, but her surprise made the question fly from her mouth before she could stop it.

A Lady's Doubt

Head cocked, he sat back and stared at the clear sky. "I believe I am. More to the point, I was enjoying the process quite a lot. Not as much as kissing you last night, mind you. Still, there is a sort of satisfaction in flirting with a woman one is fond of."

Quivering with the notion that he might actually like her, Robbie hardly knew what to say. It all came down to whether her father's actions had lured Miles in or chased him away. Either way, she didn't know if she'd ever trust in the truth of his feelings. "Are you fond of me?"

He sat forward, eyes flashing with an intensity she couldn't look away from. "I was fond of you before all this mess with our relations. Now, I see there might be hope. I have much to tell you, but this is not a long enough carriage ride for such a talk."

"What could you have learned between last night and today?" Always saying exactly what she thought was a very bad habit.

The carriage pulled to a stop in front of Collington House. Miles stepped down, waved off the footman's assistance, lowered the step and helped her down. He held her hand longer than necessary. "I will tell you everything I learned, Robbie, and then you will have to decide how we go forward."

Remaining on the step, she stood eye level with him. "Why do I get to decide?"

The corner of that full mouth tipped up and reminded her of his kiss. "Because, Robbie, I already know what I want."

Robbie had to force her mouth closed. It was possible that he actually liked her, and that was a dreamy idea. The other possibility, that the offer of land and money was too great to refuse, made her stomach roil.

The front door of Collington House opened, revealing the butler and breaking the spell Miles held over her. Climbing the steps, she tried to decide what he'd meant about knowing what he wanted. She understood he needed money and the house to get away from his brother, but he had said he would leave the money intact for any children they might have. Sylvia had said he was a good man, but how well did she really know him? Could he be lying even now?

Sylvia waited in the grand parlor. "It's good to see you both. I'm so happy you've come. Shall I call for tea?"

After a curtsy, Robbie sat on one of three chairs arranged in a row against a painted screen blocking the direct view of the door.

Miles said, "It was kind of you to include me in your visit, my lady."

A fierce frown marred Sylvia's state of amusement. "Miles Hallsmith, I will toss you from this house if you 'my lady' me one more time."

His smile launched a million butterflies to her stomach. "Forgive me, Sylvia. One never knows how to go forward after one's friends have married."

"Without you, there would have been no marriage for Tony and me. We owe you everything. You must always know that our friendship goes beyond titles and Society."

"I think the two of you would have found your way together without my help. However, it was my honor to assist." He smiled warmly, but not at all the way he smiled at Robbie.

She liked to think the sweet promising smiles he gave her were unique, even if that notion was foolish.

Tea arrived, and Sylvia poured.

Curiosity rumbled around inside Robbie until she couldn't take it anymore. She resolved not to get to know him better, as that would only make parting ways harder should his news be bad. "Is it impertinent of me to ask how Mr. Hallsmith assisted in your marriage to His Lordship?"

A Lady's Doubt

Sylvia looked askance at Miles, who said, "I have no secrets from Miss Fletcher."

It took a great deal of effort to contain her surprise, and Robbie wasn't sure she'd managed it. Everyone had secrets, and Miles hardly knew her. If he truly had no secrets, she had a lot of questions. Of course, most of them would be impolite.

"Tony and I had been separated by circumstances. He was in a terrible accident and had gone to the country to recover. I was taking you to balls and seeing to my other Everton duties. We had a great many misconceptions and unknowns holding us apart. I had just learned that my belief in Tony's indifference might be incorrect, and Miles offered to convey me and Lady Chervil to the country. Miles was a great advocate for our union and even came to Scotland with us to attend the wedding." Sylvia glowed with joy.

That expression of utter happiness was what Robbie wanted most in the world. She wanted to think of someone and feel elated and have them feel the same when they thought of her. She gnawed on her thumbnail. Father ruined everything. "That was very kind of you, Mr. Hallsmith."

He fidgeted and clasped his hands in his lap. "It was a small thing to do for friends. Plus, I truly believe Tony would have come to you as soon as he was able."

A contented sigh fell from Sylvia's lips. "Perhaps, but I like our story just as it is."

It was clear that Sylvia liked and trusted Miles, but Robbie didn't know if her friend's admiration was enough to tempt her. Her father's involvement generated a great deal of risk. She wished she'd been braver and accepted Miles's offer to walk in the park but wishing wouldn't make it so. Miles wouldn't speak of what he'd learned in front of Sylvia. Yet, whatever he'd learned could change a life she was just settling into.

Drat the entire situation.

Sylvia asked, "Robbie, what is your current Everton assignment?"

Thank goodness for safer ground. "I have three clients I help with correspondence or understanding the accounts of their estates. The Everton carriage is picking me up in thirty minutes to carry me to Lady Gracepan's home. I write letters, both personal and of a business nature, for her twice a week."

Miles frowned, maybe because she worked or because he would not be escorting her home, but she didn't like having put the expression on his handsome face.

Sylvia smiled. "I miss Everton's so much. I loved working, though I'm very happy to be married and settled. It was a wonderful few months of full independence. I think having several assignments at once is quite stimulating."

With his deep frown and stiff back, Miles looked ready to bolt.

Robbie's heart sank. She forced her fingers away from her mouth and returned her attention to Sylvia. "I enjoy the work and have learned quite a bit about the business of being a rich widow."

Miles asked, "Do you imagine having need of those skills?"

A giggle escaped. She supposed it had come out rather odd. "One never knows."

She nearly jumped when he stood and bowed. "I must be going. I have an appointment this morning."

"Come and see me more often, Miles." Sylvia said.

"I will. I promise." He stared at Robbie for a long moment but said nothing.

When he was gone, Sylvia moved next to Robbie. "I think he's in love with you."

"Nonsense. He might want to marry me, but his reasons have nothing to do with sentiment." Robbie wished it was different, but he had been offered a living, and he was taking advantage. It wasn't terrible, merely disappointing.

"I think you're wrong. Miles is not the kind of man to feign any emotion. When, for a moment, he thought of marrying me, he made no pretense of affection. He liked me and wanted to protect me. You should not toss aside his love, especially since I can see you are in love with him, too."

Robbie's heart pounded so hard it was difficult to think. "I like him. He is a nice man. We have not spent enough time together to put such a strong label on my emotions."

"Then you must spend more time with him. Invite him to dinner at Everton House." Sylvia smiled and finished her tea.

"I can't invite a man to dine at Everton House."

Frowning, Sylvia folded her hands in her lap. "Perhaps not. However, you know someone who can. If you told the entire truth to Lady Jane, I have little doubt she would assist you."

It was outrageous. "You think Lady Jane Everton would help me find out if Miles Hallsmith is a suitable match? Why would she do that?"

Sylvia's smile was sweet and knowing. "Because it's a good thing to do, and Lady Jane is the best person I have ever known. She will want what's best for you, and if that happens to be Miles, then she'll help you. If it turns out to be a bad choice, she'll stand beside you to mop up the mess."

It was an outrageous idea. Yet throughout the rest of Robbie's day, she could think of little else.

The following Thursday an extra place was set at the Everton table. Robbie was caught between excitement and worrying the dinner invitation had been a terrible mistake. Fortunately, only three other Everton ladies were home to bear witness if the meal was a complete disaster.

The two dowagers and Lady Jane were a bit less predictable. Lady Honoria Chervil would no doubt make a fuss, though Mrs. Mary Horthorn tended toward quiet and reserved. Still, Robbie wished she could give everyone a script and make them say the right things throughout the evening.

She checked the table for the third time. The best china gleamed white alongside sparkling crystal goblets and polished silver.

Ann stepped in. "What is it you're so nervous about, Robbie?"

"What if he thinks I'm a ninny?" It was the best she could make out of the hundred worries she'd allowed to roll through her mind for three days.

"Then I expect he'll spend a pleasant evening and go about his life, and you yours. However, you are not a ninny, and he is not likely to think anything of the sort. If you remain here at Everton's, you'll be no worse off than you were two weeks ago.

It was true. She had everything she needed at the Everton Domestic Society. It was a good family to be part of, and without the judgment and expectations of her relations. "You're right. I don't know what I'm fussing about. Mr. Hallsmith was invited to dinner, and he said he would come. It's not as if we're forcing him into the situation."

Typically serious and direct, Ann smiled playfully. "Exactly. Now, since he arrived ten minutes ago, perhaps you'd like to join the party in the grand parlor."

"Oh, Ann. Why didn't you say so?" Robbie ran toward the door.

"Stop," Ann commanded. "Calm yourself."

Robbie froze several feet inside the dining room. She took a deep breath. "Maybe I am a ninny."

Ann threaded her arm through Robbie's "You are just nervous because you like him. I understand. However, you are also an Everton Lady, and that requires a bit of restraint and decorum. So, take one more breath, and we'll walk together down the hall to join the others."

The breath Robbie drew was shaky and short. Even so, she gave a nod, and they strode to the parlor where the residents of Everton House gathered each night before dinner to discuss the events of the day.

Ladies were gathered around Miles, and a wave of jealousy swamped Robbie. Then as if sensing her presence, he looked up, and his expression transformed from pleasantness to elation.

Warmth seeped deep into her bones. She wanted to run into his arms but held the desire in check before she made a fool of herself in public. If she combusted on the spot, it would have been no surprise.

With a bow, he excused himself from the Everton ladies and dowagers and strode toward her.

Knees shaking, Robbie made her curtsy. "It was good of you to come, Mr. Hallsmith."

"I was honored to receive an invitation." His smile nearly had her swooning like one of those silly women in dramatic novels.

Refusing to be ridiculous, she reined in her emotions. "You know my friend, Miss Ann Wittman?"

"Of course, good to see you again, Miss Wittman."

Ann curtsied. "A pleasure. If you will both excuse me, I

must speak to Lady Chervil."

Covering a smile, Miles stood next to Robbie. "I really was pleased to receive the invitation. After our last meeting, I was unsure if you wished to see me again."

"Because I had to attend to business?"

He turned so that he blocked the rest of the room and gave them a bit of privacy. "Not at all. Because you seemed distracted, and you had not informed me that I would not be escorting you home. When I was invited to tea, I still believed you and I would have time to talk.

"I believed it wiser to arrange another means of transport as I had clients to attend to."

He shook his head, disappointed glinting in his eyes. "You made other arrangements either because you did not want to be in my company or because you did not wish to hear what I had learned. If the first, then this invitation to dinner makes little sense. If the second, I would like to hear why you were frightened."

"Not afraid exactly."

"No? What would you call it?" Concern and warmth shone in his eyes.

"If you told me something unspeakable it might end our odd courtship. I'm not ready to see this come to an end." She really was a complete ninny. She searched the room for an appropriate haven. Spotting Ann and Lady Chervil, she moved to stepped around him.

"Please don't run from me, Robbie," Miles whispered.

His soft pleading stopped her in her tracks. Looking into those striking blue eyes, she was frozen in his spell.

Miles closed his eyes and took a long breath. His eyes filled with longing as he stared into hers. "On our last meeting, I sensed you wished me away, and so I complied. I'm glad to hear you didn't wish me away permanently."

A Lady's Doubt

Had her demeanor been so stoic as to chase him away? It was foolish to deny that she liked Miles Hallsmith, but Father's involvement... "Forgive me. Perhaps when you tell me more of what you know regarding the arrangement between my father and your brother, I will be more at ease with our situation."

He reached out as if to touch her cheek, then pulled back before exposing such an intimacy to everyone in the parlor. "Do you think Lady Jane would disapprove of us having a private meeting after dinner?"

"It would be highly irregular, but if the door is left open, I cannot see her troubling over it."

"Then I will tell you all that I know after dinner."

Lord Rupert and Lady Jane entered and greeted Miles. The conversation turned to the fine weather and other nonsense.

What followed was the longest meal of Robbie's entire life. It was not until the group returned to the grand parlor for cake that she and Miles were permitted to meet in the small parlor.

As soon as she walked in, all her arguments to never marry reverberated hollow in her mind. Here was a man who might actually like her, and she had offered him nothing but doubt in return. Sweat dotted her forehead, and her hands became clammy.

Remaining near the door, Miles waited for her to sit, stared at her for a moment, then said, "You look as if I'm about to flay you alive, Robbie."

She stood and crossed to the window. "I don't know why I'm so nervous. You have not misled me or given me cause to mistrust you. In fact, you have been generous and honest in a very awkward situation."

"Yet you are uneasy about me?" he said, his voice tight with regret.

"No. You see, for some time, I believed I knew what I

wanted. This situation has challenged those notions." She couldn't lie to herself. She liked Miles, and if it were not for his coming because of an arrangement, she would have been flattered by his attention.

His eyes filled with delight. "I understand. Come and sit, please."

Nothing would give her more pleasure than putting that joy in his eyes every day. The fact settled deep in her belly and spread outward filling her. She'd fallen and there was not returning from the spill.

Once seated beside her, he smiled. "My brother has a vote in the House of Lords, which it seems your father covets. After a short investigation, I believe your father is collecting votes to keep the abolition of carrying slaves to the new world from passing."

"What?" Robbie's stomach knotted, and she thought she might lose what little dinner she'd forced down.

Taking her hand from her lap, he caressed her knuckles. "I know. It's not what you wanted to hear about your father. Believe me, I'm ashamed that my brother would consider selling his vote for a parcel of land."

"A parcel of land and your future happiness," Robbie said. Nothing made sense, yet it all did. Father had many businesses that grew on the backs of slaves and shipping those poor souls west. She'd tried many times to make him see the harm he did, but he was blind with greed.

"True, my brother has little concern for my well-being. Luckily, I don't believe my happiness is at stake, Robbie. And I'd like to believe I could make you happy as well. However, I can't allow my brother to hide behind this marriage arrangement. I think we must expose them." He said it as one might speak of a bad meal.

"I'm confused." Perhaps he'd changed his mind. Of course,

he had. He could expose Father and his brother and be done with the entire mess. "Can we take each of these issues separately?"

There again was that smile that muddled her mind. "You may do anything you like, sweetheart. You are in control of our futures."

"Am I?"

"Of course." He kissed the inside of her wrist.

Unable to think while he touched her, she pulled her hand away. "Do you want to marry me, and I don't mean because of land and a house? If those things were not part of this, would you have any interest in Roberta Fletcher, Everton Lady?"

"Oh, Robbie, how is it you don't know how perfect you are? Yes. I would want you to share my life no matter the circumstances. Never doubt that. However, without the house and property, I would not have the means or the right to ask you to be mine." Sincerity and regret rang in his voice and shone in his eyes.

Staring at the rug's flower design, she avoided returning to his gaze. Her hands trembled, so she gripped the cushion to steady herself. Still, not knowing was worse than her current level of embarrassment, which was far worse than any she'd ever known. "But—and forgive me for being so blunt—do you think you could love me?"

Miles went to his knees in front of her. He gently disengaged her death grip from the divan cushion and took both her hands in his. "If you will let me, I will love you for all the days of my life, Robbie. You are beautiful and smart, funny and brave. I have admired you since the first time we met. I would have courted you then if I'd had the right to do so. I don't know how we will manage our situation, but if you are willing, I truly, and without reservation, want to be your husband."

She'd thought he'd be polite and say something appropriate,

but he loved her. Her chest filled with emotion, she couldn't breathe, and she imagined dying on the spot. "You love me?"

He leaned close and whispered, "I do."

Those two tiny words, said so intimately, sent a thrill through her. "I never dreamed you would love me. Well, maybe I dreamed it in the way one dreams of the impossible."

He kissed her left hand then her right. "I promise this is not a dream, though if you'll agree to be mine, I might think it one as well."

It was not practical to say yes, but perhaps love should be accepted on a whim with no secure future. "If we marry, my father will get your brother's vote. What if we are the cause of continued suffering for so many?"

"I have no intention of allowing my brother to abuse his vote."

Flooded with relief, Robbie sighed. "But if you refuse, how would we live?"

"Do you love me, Robbie?"

"Yes, but that is not enough to feed us, and what of our children?"

The music in his laughter filled her with happiness she'd never imagined possible. "I have a plan to get everything we want and keep your father from succeeding in his horrible plan. However, because he is your father, I need your approval and assistance."

Excitement bubbled inside her. "You should get off your knees and tell me everything."

"First tell me you'll marry me."

"Of course, I'll marry you." Pure bliss rolled out with the words.

Miles rose, lifting her with him. Despite the open door, and the residents of Everton House just down the hall, he kissed her until her knees wobbled.

Chapter Five

For his plan to work, Miles would have to time everything perfectly. The Everton carriage stood in the street as he pulled up to his brother's townhouse. Robbie being inside made everything worthwhile. However, the idea that she was enduring her father's company had Miles taking the steps two at a time.

A new butler opened the door. "Good morning, sir."

"Good morning. Forgive me, you are?"

"Travis, sir."

"I shall not forget again, Travis. I hope things are going well for you." In the past, Miles would have handled a new hire, but he'd stepped back in the past few weeks.

Travis nodded stiffly. "Everything is satisfactory, sir. Thank you for asking."

"I'm glad to hear it." Miles had made sure the retired butler was properly pensioned. It would have been just like Ford to leave the man with nothing after twenty years of service. Miles hoped that would be the last work he would ever do for his brother.

"Your mother, brother and the Fletcher family await you in the study," Travis said.

For all of his adult life, Miles had thought keeping his brother out of trouble and taking care of the family accounts was a lark and not a bad way to live for a third son. Yet once freedom and Robbie's heart were dangled before him, he wanted those things more than breath.

Without knocking, Miles opened the study door.

Roberson Fletcher hovered over Robbie. "You will do as I say, Roberta. You have disobeyed me for the last time."

As beautiful as ever, Robbie sighed without responding. She leaned on her fist, and her elbow rested on the arm of the overstuffed chair.

Her mother, Lenora Fletcher, sat in the other chair, smiling as if her greatest day had arrived. She seemed impervious to her husband's blathering or her daughter's misery.

Behind his desk, Ford squinted at a page, which meant he wasn't certain about the meaning.

Mother stood and crossed to Miles. Her red hair was pulled into a loose bun. Streaks of gray running through were the only indication of her age. She kissed his cheek, and whispered, "Are you certain about all of this?"

Roberson barked, "Sit up straight. You're not the baker's daughter. I swear, I have no idea where you got such bad habits. It certainly wasn't from your mother or me."

Mother rolled her eyes, giving Miles the impression Roberson had been at this for some time.

"Don't worry, Mother. I am most definitely doing the right thing." Miles patted her hand and fully entered the room. "Good morning. I'm happy to see everyone is here."

"Good. Miles, read this." Ford held the betrothal agreement out toward him.

Ignoring Ford, Miles turned to Robbie. "It's good to see you again, Miss Fletcher."

She stood and curtsied. "And you, Mr. Hallsmith. My father tells me the documents are all in order. I hope they will be acceptable to you."

"Your agreement honors me." It wasn't easy to hide his elation, and when she blushed, it took all his effort to remain serious. It wouldn't do to give away the plan before the game was won.

After greeting her parents, he took the contract from Ford, walked to the small writing desk in the corner where he often worked, and read the betrothal contract.

It was full of contradictions and poor wording. It gave him the property he wanted then took it away two pages later. It left nothing for his children, should he have any. Miles wished he could say he was surprised, but it was exactly what he'd expected from his brother.

"My attorney will be here momentarily. There are some small points I wish changed in the wording. He will make those changes and witness the signing." He'd used the calm unaffected tone a million times with his brother. It was normal, and he hated it.

Fletcher's face turned bright red. "This is a family matter. There is no reason to bring a stranger in. The contract is perfect as it is."

Drawing close to Roberson Fletcher, Miles lowered his voice. "As much as I admire your daughter, I must be allowed to support her and any children that might come from the marriage. This contract is unacceptable."

"You would fleece your own brother?"

Ford sat up straight and pounded his fist on the desk. "I demand you sign."

"I will not. And if you are wise, Ford, you will have the

attorney check the papers for the land agreement you're entering into with Mr. Fletcher as well."

As Ford looked at the stack of papers on his desk, his bluster faltered. "It might be a good idea."

"We had an agreement, Hallsmith." Spittle flew from Fletcher's mouth.

With a slow smile, Ford sat back. "We agreed that if my brother married your disobedient daughter, you would give me her dowry plus the land that abuts Thornbury. In order to make that transaction appealing to my brother, I forfeit the dowry to him and gave him a very good piece of land with a house. I think I have been more than fair."

From the doorway, Jonathan Wakefield cleared his throat. "Pardon my interruption, my lord. Your butler told me to come right in."

Miles made the introductions to his attorney and friend. He'd run many documents past Mr. Wakefield over the years to ensure his brother was neither being cheated nor cheating anyone. Miles had always thought it best to keep their association to himself, until this situation arose.

"I overheard your very fine summary of the agreement, my lord. Was there anything you wished to add, Mr. Fletcher?" Wakefield took the contract from Miles.

Ford handed over the other contract as well.

Bright red, with cheeks puffed out, Fletcher looked about to burst. "No. Those were the contracted agreements. But I am very put out by this private matter being scrutinized so intently. Where is the trust?"

Taking a quill and ink from Ford's desk, Wakefield went to the desk and began marking the contracts.

Miles said, "I would like a moment alone, Mr. Fletcher. Would you join me in the corridor for a moment?"

A Lady's Doubt

"In the corridor? This is highly unusual." Fletcher crossed to the door.

"Yes. I apologize. It is odd, but I think that is the perfect place for what I have to say." Miles followed him out.

Robbie smiled at him and nodded her approval. It was just the fortification he needed to do what must be done.

Once he'd closed the study door, Miles checked for servants. Finding the hallway empty, he whispered, "I noticed you have already signed the contracts, Mr. Fletcher."

"Of course. I saw nothing wrong with them." He fisted his hands and crossed his arms over his chest.

Miles leaned in close and kept his voice low, yet it still held all the warning he needed. "Good. I will marry your daughter. I'm happy and honored she has agreed. You, however, will not get what you want. My brother's vote is not for sale. Not only that, I think you will find that many of the peers you have bribed will be backing out of their agreements with you. I would not want my wife embarrassed by your behavior, so I have been very discreet. However, both Roberta and I have agreed that should you continue your abhorrent behavior, we will expose you. I doubt a scandal about buying votes will sit well with your creditors."

"You fiend. How dare you?" Fletcher's raised voice brought maids and footmen running.

Miles smiled. "Not to worry. All is well. Shall we go back inside and finalize the happy occasion?"

"I'll not sign!"

Pushing the door open, Miles smiled into the face of the man who would soon be his father-in-law. "Ah, but you already have, sir."

Standing at the desk, Robbie put down the quill she'd used to sign the betrothal contract, smiled warmly and lifted a bright gaze toward him.

Miles strode over, took her hand and kissed it. "Is everything to your liking?"

With a narrowed glance at her father, she huffed out a sigh. When she returned her attention to Miles, her smile returned. "It will all be perfect as soon as you sign."

Heart leaping in his chest, he hated to let go of her hand. Miles took up the quill and placed his name next to Robbie's on a document promising they'd spend their lives together.

Clapping, Mrs. Fletcher leapt up. "I'm so thrilled." She hugged Robbie and babbled about how she'd always known her daughter would make a good match.

They were like actors performing their parts in a scene from a poorly written Covent Garden play.

Father should have been ashamed, but once his plot was foiled, he sulked in the corner.

She clung to the only real thing, her adoration for Miles, and based on the way he looked at her, his feelings mirrored her own. After such a messy year, she was in love. It sounded impossible, but the burst of joy inside her said it was true.

By all accounts, Ford Hallsmith was as bad as her father, but he seemed genuinely pleased by the outcome. Perhaps he was happy he'd gotten away with something. Robbie hoped it was more because his brother would be happy.

It was still morning when the transaction was finalized. It had been nice to meet Miles's mother. Lady Lucretia was kind and accepted her with open arms.

Mother gathered her reticule and shawl and was tying the bow of her flowery bonnet.

Panic settled in Robbie's gut at the thought of leaving Miles. She didn't know why it should bother her. She could take care of herself. Still, she wanted him near and worried he would come to his senses and break their agreement.

In her head she knew he would never do so. Miles was a good man, honest and noble. He would not betray her.

Mother's singsong voice rang out. "Oh Roberta, you will come home, be married from there, and all will be well again."

Going home to listen to her father complain about Miles for the next two and a half months while the banns were read was a torture Robbie could not endure. "I see no reason to change my living arrangements. Besides, I will need to give Lady Jane proper notice of my impending marriage. Each of my clients will have to be cared for and assigned to other Everton Ladies. No. It is best I stay where I am."

"I won't hear of it." Father stormed over, his face bright red and his eyes wild.

Robbie stepped back, stumbling on a chair leg.

Miles wrapped an arm around her waist, pulled her upright, and stepped between her and Father. "You are going to have to quell your temper around my betrothed, sir. I am in agreement with Miss Fletcher. She should stay at Everton House, where she is safe and happy. If you wish to put in the paper that she is married out of your townhouse or country estate, I will leave that entirely up to you."

Even Ford had risen during the commotion.

Mother said, "Oh dear." Her eyes were wide, and she chewed her bottom lip. "Perhaps Roberta is right. It was only that I wanted to spend more time with my girl before she leaves me forever."

Tears popped into Robbie's eyes. She hated that her mother had been caught in the middle of her father's plans. It hurt her to see Mother distressed. She stepped around the men and pulled her mother into a hug. "I will come for tea as often as I can."

Father stormed from the study.

"I think that went as well as it could." Ford straightened his jacket and left.

Miles cleared his throat. "Perhaps the three of us might take my carriage out to the house in Surrey and tour the grounds. See what needs to be repaired? Mother, perhaps you would like to join us as well."

"I would be delighted. I have always liked that cottage." Lucretia gave her youngest son a warm smile.

Keeping one arm around Mother, Robbie looked through watery eyes at the kindest man in all of England. "You wouldn't mind?"

"It would be my honor." He bowed, his smile wide and infectious. "In fact, I think in the next ten weeks, the four of us should make the trip several times, just to be sure everything is to your liking, Robbie. Mr. Fletcher will have much work here and likely be unable to accompany us, but we shall make do."

Mother's gaze flitted around the room before settling on Robbie. "You wouldn't mind taking the time off from the Everton Domestic Society?"

"No, Mother. I would not mind at all. It would only be a few days at a time."

Clapping, Mother beamed. "Then I think it a wonderful idea. Can we leave directly?"

"Will tomorrow be soon enough, madam?" Miles asked. "It is only thirty miles, but some preparations and packing will be required."

"Perfect." Her mother kissed his cheek and walked out, humming happily.

"I'll just see Mrs. Fletcher to the front door." Lady Lucretia giggled and stepped out of the study.

Euphoria erupted inside Robbie. After a quick check for

anyone at the door, she rushed into Miles's arms. "You are too good to me."

Holding her and caressing her back, he pressed a kiss to the top of her head. "It is nothing, and mostly done out of my selfish desire to spend more time with you."

"Whatever your reasons, it made my mother very happy." She snuggled against his chest, giddy with the notion she would have leave to revel in his warm woodsy scent for the rest of her life."

"And you, Robbie. Do I make you happy?" A rumble of concern edged his voice.

Standing in his arms was a kind of heaven she'd never thought to have. Nothing could have prepared her for how wonderful her life had turned out. "You and I are going to have the happiest marriage the world has ever seen."

"How do you know?"

She pulled away to look at him. "Just from what you did today, Miles. Stopped Father's plans, made Mother rapturously happy, stood by me and my decisions without flinching, and did all of that without compromising your own values. You are a remarkable man. How could you not make me the happiest of women?"

Miles ran his knuckles along her jaw to her chin. "I did what any man would do to win the woman he loves."

Joyous tears threatened. "Truly, I think you won me long before our relatives tried to spoil everything. I've loved you from the moment we met, Miles Hallsmith. I was only waiting for you to find your way to me."

"Now that I have, it shall be a rare thing that I let you out of my sight." He pulled her back into his embrace and kissed her.

Robbie sank into the kiss. From the foyer, her father's raised voice broke the spell, even though whatever he said was lost to the distance.

Sighing, Robbie pulled away. "I shall never have to hide away to keep safe from the machinations of others again. It is a strange notion, but one I shall get used to."

Hand in hand, they walked toward the commotion in the foyer. "You and I have never had much freedom on our own, my love. That is about to change. In ten short weeks, we will be entirely free to do as we please."

Robbie longed to explore all the new possibilities in her life, but only as long as that journey was with Miles.

Read the complete series now:

A Lady's Honor
A Lady's Escape
A Lady's Virtue
A Lady's Doubt
A Lady's Past

Turn the page to read the first chapter of A Lady's Past.

A Lady's Past

The greatest risk—for the sweetest reward...

His fiancée's betrayal nearly cost Jacques Laurent everything. Despite his resolve not to trust anyone again, he can't abandon the young woman he finds alone on the road to London. In the brief hours they spend together, the enigmatic Diana touches his heart in a way he can't explain. Even after bringing her to the Everton Domestic Society for safekeeping, he can't get her out of his thoughts. And when he next encounters her, working as assistant to a renowned scientist, he becomes even more intrigued...

The Society's kindness is especially welcome after everything Diana endured in a French prison, but she fears for the safety of those who get close to her. French spies are on her trail, convinced that her scientific knowledge can help them win the war. As peril draws them irrevocably together, Diana and Jacques succumb to mutual desire. But love may be the most dangerous pursuit of all, when a lady guards her heart even more carefully than she guards her life...

CHAPTER ONE

Wet roads, a carriage that needed new springs, a relentless drizzle, and still Jacques Laurent had enjoyed one of the best days he'd had in a long time. Seeing his parents safe in England, after worrying about their fate in France all these years, was a relief beyond measure. If not for an important meeting in London the following morning, he would have stayed a few more days in the country.

Now that he had their well-being to worry about too, he could ill afford to miss an opportunity to increase his accounts.

His small covered carriage did little to protect him from the drizzle, and even less as it turned to a light snow. One never could predict November. He pulled the collar of his coat tighter.

Something large and gray darted into the trees on the side of the road. Pulling back on the reins, Jacques squinted into the dense woods. "I saw you, so if you have plans to attack me, you may as well show yourself.

I am well armed and not the least bit worried about dispatching a villain tonight, though it would ruin a perfectly good day."

The leaves rustled, and someone cleared her throat.

Jacques's curiosity was piqued. He'd never met a female highwayman. Would they be called a highwaywoman? He would give it thought, but later. Her gun barrel preceded her out of the shadows into the dusk of evening.

Hair the color of the richest coffee tumbled around her shoulders as her cape caught on a low branch. "I am also not afraid to shoot. Are you a spy?" Her question was not unusual.

His French accent had provoked the notion more than once. It was the times, and nothing could be done about it until the unrest passed. "Certainly not. Spies do not dress well, and they keep terrible hours. The question is, why would a lady such as yourself be traveling alone at night and on foot? More importantly and far more interestingly, why do you concern yourself with spies rather than highwaymen and murderers?"

She raised the barrel of her shotgun and looked at him through the threads. "I'm not in a position to answer any of those questions. You should be on your way." She motioned down the road with the weapon while keeping her cheek against the butt and her finger on the trigger.

Chest tight, he sighed. "I'm afraid I cannot leave you here, madam." "Why on earth not?" Her nose scrunched up in the most adorable way.

Wishing he could discern the color of her eyes, he squinted to try to make them out. Blue, perhaps, but the light was dim with the late hour and persistent snow. "I am a gentleman."

"And that means you can't leave a total stranger to her own devices?" A hint of amusement filtered into her voice.

There was something compelling about the low, raspy tone. "Were you running into or out of town?"

She huffed. "I'm not running."

"I suspect this is a falsehood, but it is none of my business."

"That much is true." She pressed the gun's butt tighter to the crease of her shoulder.

Laughing, he said, "If you are willing to stop pointing the dangerous end of that weapon at me, I would be happy to convey you into London and drop you wherever you wish."

She lowered the gun, her bravado faltering. Her eyes cast down, she pursed her lips. "I will bash you on the head with this if you so much as look like you will attack me."

"Noted." He took both reins in one hand and offered her

the other to climb up. Once she was seated, he clucked to Midas and the horse trotted on. "You may leave me at Parliament or Piccadilly, whichever is more convenient to you." Weapon across her lap and no luggage, now her bravado failed, and she might have been a lost puppy rather than the bold woman

of a moment before.

It tugged at something inside Jacques that a woman with an education, from the sound of her voice, had come to be alone on the road several hours outside of London with nothing but a shotgun. He had a suspicion. "If you have no place to stay tonight, I can offer you my townhouse or perhaps take you to the home of one of my married friends. The Duke and Duchess of Middleton would be happy to take care of you this evening."

Shoulders back, she stared straight ahead. "That is very kind, but unnecessary. I will be fine."

The snow came down harder. "I am sure that is true. What is your name?" The silence stretched out until he was sure she would refuse to answer.

Then, her voice barely a whisper on the wind, she said, "Diana."

Why her name should make him grin, he had no idea. "Yet there is no moon."

"I beg your pardon?"

He kept his attention on the road but felt her looking at him. "Your name. Diana, goddess of the hunt and the moon."

"Yes, well, my father was fond of mythology."

A tiny noose tightened around his heart. It was absurd. "And your father is no longer with you?"

It was a straight bit of road, and he turned his head in time to see her frown and the tightening of her full lips. She reached up and pulled her hair back, twisting it into a knot at her nape.

"My father died a year ago." "I'm very sorry. I am Jacques Laurent. Have you any family to whom

I might deliver you this evening?" Already sensing the answer, he wanted her to say something positive and comforting. The idea of her being alone in the world gnawed at him.

"No. I have no family. You may drop me at one of my previously stated locations." Her back was straight as an oak, and she stared ahead into the waning gray day. Snow speckled her dark hair. Pulling her hood up, she hid her beauty.

It wouldn't do to pull the hood back and demand she let him see her. He sighed. The places she'd requested to be left were both heavily frequented. She chose spots where she would not be alone. Obviously, she needed the crowd for protection. But who was she afraid of?

None of his business was the mantra he repeated in his head. He would drop her in the city, go to bed, attend his meeting in the morning and then head back to the country with his friends. The Duke and Duchess of Middleton were anxious to visit with his parents. Preston had been his friend since birth, as their fathers had attended school together. They would collect the dowager duchess and head back to Crestwood, the small estate he'd purchased for his parents. He'd left them with a competent staff, but he hated the notion of them being alone after their long journey.

His friends had recently married after meeting when Millie was hired through the Everton Domestic Society to be Preston's matchmaker. It was no time at all before the matchmaker became matched. Jacques liked Millie; she was smart and funny and the perfect wife for the serious Duke of Middleton.

It was an early first snow. The wind picked up and the chill seeped through his coat. He imagined Diana was freezing in that light cape.

She pulled the edges closer around her neck, and her teeth chattered together in cadence with the rumble of the wheels. The snow was making it harder and harder to see, and the horse misstepped, pulling the carriage sideways.

Diana gave a short yelp and grabbed the seat.

Jacques couldn't blame her. They had come inches from running off the road. "I think there is a small inn or a farmhouse up ahead. I assume you will not be keen on the idea, but we have to stop for the night and hope the weather clears by morning."

Her shoulders lifted then sank with a long sigh, and she gave him a nod. The inn was indeed small, and a bit worse for wear. Jacques immediately doubted the wisdom of stopping at such a place with a lady, but they had little choice. Neither he nor Midas could continue.

As soon as they stopped, a round-bellied man in a robe and nightcap rushed into the yard. "Lord, what a night. I expect you two got caught up. Come in. Leave the horse. I'll have young Robbie take the beast for feed and shelter. He'll give him a good rubdown as well. Come in, come in out of the cold. Mrs. Tinker has water boiling for tea."

Jacques secured the reins and turned to Diana. "It seems we are welcome for a bit of an adventure."

The smile she graced him with nearly toppled him from the seat. "It would seem so."

He was going to have to get himself under control. This woman was nothing to him, and he would do well to remember that. Offering his hand, he helped her down from the carriage. He leaned close to her ear. "I shall have to give him a false name and tell him we're married. I assume you have a reputation to protect regardless of your current situation, and you would not wish to be forced to marry me."

"Heavens, no." Wide-eyed, she truly looked horrified.

"You wound me with the quickness of your reply." He joked, but her decisive rejection gnawed at him.

Cocking her head, she studied him, then turned and followed the waving innkeeper into the building. "Thank you for allowing us to bother you so late on such a night."

The innkeeper bowed. "Benjamin Tinker at your service, madam. We have only one guest tonight, so you and your husband are a welcome addition. I'm relieved you found your way in the storm."

"I'll take you up directly and Mrs. Tinker will bring you your tea. You must be in need of a rest. When we heard the carriage, I took the liberty of having Robbie start a fire in one of our guest rooms. Anyone out tonight will be chilled to the bone." He nodded to Jacques and ambled up the steep stairs.

The inn was small and worn, but clean. Two tables and a small bar made up the common area. A door that probably led to the family quarters was at the far end, and a smell that reminded him of his cook's stew filtered out. At the top of the stairs, a short hall revealed three doors.

Tinker took them to the last one and the hinges squealed as he opened it. He lit a lantern on the table and adjusted the flame. "I'm afraid this is the best we have. We don't usually get such a fine clientele. I hope it will be all right." He set about feeding the fire in the small hearth.

Sparsely furnished, the room had a bed, a chair and a table. A small trunk sat at the end of the bed. The window out to the yard was freshly cleaned and revealed a young lad cooing to Midas and leading him off toward a barn with the door half off the hinges.

Jacques had stayed in far worse places in his lifetime. He handed a shilling to their host. "This is perfect, Mr. Tinker. I cannot thank you enough."

Elated with the early payment, Mr. Tinker beamed. "If you

need anything at all, we live off the kitchen downstairs. We're happy to help." "Thank you." Jacques walked him to the door and closed it behind him. "This is cozy."

"I will sleep on the floor, Mr. Laurent." She'd leaned the shotgun against the wall and removed her hood, then stood with her cape tightly wrapped around her as if it would shield her from him. The lamplight revealed crystal-blue eyes pale against her warm, creamy skin and mahogany hair. "The hell you will. I might not be English, but I'll not sleep in the bed while you lie on the cold floor. You may have the bed, and I will manage with the chair."

Those full, rosy lips opened as if to protest when someone scratched on the door.

Jacques opened it to a lady in a voluminous robe and cap. Her mousy brown hair poked out from under the threadbare cap, but her faded blue eyes were filled with joy. "I've got tea and stew. I thought you might be hungry after traveling through the weather. You both look wet through. There are extra blankets in that trunk, and I brought you warm water for washing."

"Thank you, Mrs. Tinker. You are most kind."

"Anything you need, you just ask." She blushed and rushed out.

Diana opened the trunk and removed a quilt made with scraps of dozens of materials. The most charming blush lit her cheeks. "I would be grateful if you would hold this while I take off this wet dress."

Suddenly the idea of a naked goddess Diana, complete with bow and arrows, forced its way into his ungentlemanly head. Forcing down his baser thoughts, he bolted the door and accepted the quilt. "Of course."

"This is most awkward."

He held the blanket up high enough that he couldn't see

through it. Cloth rustled on the other side. "It is better than freezing to death on the road tonight."

Taking the quilt from him, she wrapped it around herself. Eyes like starlight filled with worry. "I'm not ungrateful, Mr. Laurent. Your timing in picking me up could not have been better. I had planned to search for a hunter's shack or some shelter for the night. This is far better. I only meant that taking one's clothes off while a total stranger held a quilt up was quite awkward."

"I knew what you meant. This has been quite an evening." His laugh rolled out without warning. His stomach growled.

She laughed too. "What do you do, sir?"

"Since I don't know your last name, you should call me Jacques. I invest in inventions and import goods." He spooned some stew and reveled in the rich flavors and unexpected spice. English food was generally bland to his taste. "This is good."

Crossing with one hand clutching the blanket, she sat and ate the stew as if it had been days since she'd eaten. Nothing about this woman added up. "What do you do, Diana?"

"Why would you assume I do anything? Ladies don't have occupations." He slid the bowl with his remaining stew across to her.

After a brief hesitation, she devoured that as well before picking up her tea and sipping.

"I do not think you are like other ladies. I suspect you have a past that would be most interesting to hear about. Perhaps one day you will tell me what sent you out into the cold with nothing but a cloak and a shotgun." Sipping his tea, he watched her expressionless face. She'd been scared when they were in the carriage, and she'd let her fear show. Now, in the warm inn with a full belly, she wore a mask of indifference that seemed well practiced.

"My circumstances are hardly your concern." She put

down the tea and slipped into the bed. Watching him with wide eyes that betrayed her mistrust, her mask slipped, and she looked like a lost child.

He wanted to give her comfort, but of course, she was right. "No. If you would turn your head, I would like to get out of these wet clothes and put on something dry. I would have offered you a shirt, but you seem content with that mummification you created."

She did as he wished, a dark blush creeping into her cheek.

Once he was in a dry pair of trousers and a blouse, he hung their clothes over the chair and the two hooks in the wall near the fire, so they would perhaps dry by morning. Stoking the fire, he watched her and tried to decide if she would rob him in his sleep or slit his throat.

With a sigh, he doused the lamp and pulled two blankets from the trunk. He made a pallet on the floor near the hearth, lay down, and put his hands behind his head. If she was a murderess and thief, so be it. He was too tired to worry.

"Jacques?"

"Yes, Diana?" His heart sped up at the rasp of her voice in the darkness. "Can I trust you?" Her back was to him, leaving him to wonder at her

expression. Her inflection told him nothing of her motives.

It was doubtless the oddest evening he'd ever spent. "I believe you can.

I try to live honorably."

"I'm afraid." The first quaver touched her voice.

His gut twisted with worry over what scared this complete stranger. He didn't know her, but he'd formed an immediate attachment, which he couldn't explain. Sitting up, he turned toward the bed. "How can I help?" Rolling over, she faced him. The small fire revealed tears trailing down her cheeks, leaving blotchy streaks. "You don't want to know what scares me?"

"Only if my knowing will ease your immediate fears." She shook her head.

"What would?"

Her pale skin pinked, and she stared into the dark corner near the window. "It's too much to ask. Even if we knew each other it would be too much to ask."

Standing, he opened his arms wide. "If you do not ask, we shall never know."

Clutching her blanket, she sat up. "I have been alone and without friends or family for some time. I can't tell you why I am in this state, but it's been quite lonely. I wonder... That is to say... Would you be willing to hold me? And only hold me, for a short while?"

Heart tripping like one of his friend Francis's inventions before the explosions, he cleared his throat. "I... That is not what I expected you to say." He laughed.

Bright red now, she turned away and lay back down. "I apologize. It was foolish of me."

Swallowing a wave of desire, Jacques climbed into the bed. Despite her request, she stiffened like a board.

"It would be my honor to hold you until you fall asleep, Diana. You are safe with me." He placed his hand on her back and waited.

After a minute, she relaxed.

He wrapped his arms around her and pulled her close. The most annoying thought, of how perfectly she fit him, rolled through his head. His body reacted, and it required concentration to relax, as much as one could relax when holding a beautiful, mysterious woman in his arms in the middle of the night.

A long sigh escaped her lips and she relaxed against him. "I have made you uncomfortable."

It was no use denying it, as he was sure she could feel his

arousal. "Only in the most delightful way. Go to sleep, Diana. Things will seem better in the morning."

Her next breath heaved with whatever burden she carried. "Oh, how I wish that were true, Jacques."

When she said no more, he breathed in the warm scent of her and closed his eyes. It was best to let sleep take him lest he drive himself mad with curiosity.

Soft tendrils of her dark tresses slid across his cheek from where her head lay on his shoulder. Her head grew heavy and her breath even.

By far, the oddest evening to date. He closed his eyes and let the tiring day catch up with him.

Sun shone bright through the windows, making Jacques squint awake. Warm skin against his chest reminded him that he hadn't slept alone. Her hair splayed like a halo across his neck and chest, Diana slept. Her blanket had slipped precariously low, though it still covered her. Her arm hugged his waist and his wrapped around her back. Her skin was like velvet, and he longed to touch all of her.

Easing up, he shifted her to the pillow. "Diana, it is daylight. We had better pay Mr. Tinker and get to London. I have a meeting this morning." She stretched like a cat after milk and a long nap. The swell of her breast mounded over the top of the quilt, calling to him to return to the

bed and take as much delight as she had to give.

That idea of climbing back into the bed and seeing exactly what she looked like beneath that blanket warred with his good nature and gentleman's status. This was some kind of torture, he was sure. Perhaps it was penance for a misspent youth. The fire was out, but her dress was dry. He gave it to her, tucked his blouse in and finished dressing. He might have time to get home, wash and change before his meeting.

He stuffed his clothes into his bag and went to the door. "I will settle the bill while you dress. Shall I meet you at the carriage?"

Beet red, she forced that look of indifference and said, "I'll be down in a few minutes, and would appreciate the ride to town."

With a nod, Jacques left her to dress and went down to pay Mr. Tinker. He found a parcel of warm bread and cheese had been put together for their journey.

Mrs. Tinker handed it to him. "I thought you two would be wanting to continue on your way early since it was the weather that stopped you."

"You are most kind."

Jacques paid Mr. Tinker and thanked him as well, before stepping into the cool morning, where he waited for Robbie to deliver Midas and the carriage.

Midas looked fed and happy when he clomped into the yard.

Right on time, Diana stepped out of the inn, calling back her thanks as she closed the door.

The three inches of snow was already melting in the sunshine as Jacques handed her up into the carriage.

"I have been thinking about your problem of where to stay in London, and I have an idea that might serve both our sensibilities," he said as they took to the road.

She looked at him. Her blue eyes sparkled in the early morning light. "I wasn't aware I had a problem. To what sensibilities are you referring?"

The sarcasm dripping from her words forced his grin. "I do not wish to leave a lady alone on the streets of London, and you are clearly in need of a place to hide."

"Why would you think I am hiding?" She tipped her pert chin up, and the cape slipped from her head.

His longing to touch that mass of dark hair was completely inappropriate, but churned like a whirlwind inside him. He needed to take her somewhere before she got too far under his skin, then he would never think of her again. "Do not insult my intelligence, Diana. You are clearly running. Though I do not know if it is to or from something or someone. You chose locations that are dense with people so that you can hide in the crowd."

Her shoulders sagged, and she nodded. "What is your idea?"

Oh, he liked her more and more. This was a problem. Drawing a deep breath in an effort to dispel the memory of her sweet body pressed to his, he said, "I think you might get on well at the Everton Domestic Society. I could bring you there and see if Lady Jane might put you up for a few days, perhaps longer if you have some skills and you are interested in the work."

"I'm not familiar with the Everton Domestic Society." She frowned.

He tried to ignore her stiff posture. Where had she been that she wouldn't have heard of the society? Keeping his mind on the facts and getting her to safety was all he cared about. "It is very popular. Lord and Lady Everton run a business where ladies might find respectable employment as assistants in different areas. Sometimes they help young ladies with a debut. My friend's mother hired an Everton lady as a matchmaker. I understand they have many functions within the boundaries of proper society."

"Employment for ladies in London society? This sounds scandalous." Her light comment told him she was not in the least scandalized.

"It should be, but it seems to be accepted. Most of the ladies are beyond their youth and this is preferable to being a burden on their families."

Lips pursed, she stilled. "Of course, all we can be is a burden or a wife." Something about her annoyance made him smile. Actually, everything about this mystery of a woman filled him with delight. "These are not my sentiments, Diana. I know for a fact there are a great many talented and brilliant women in the world, part of the both upper class and lower. I do not make the rules by which we live. As I said, the Everton Domestic Society finds respectable employment for ladies. If you would like, I will take you to meet Lady Jane, and perhaps you can come to some understanding. If not, I will drop you in Piccadilly or wherever you choose."

She was quiet for several miles. London came into view and she stiffened. "This Society sounds intriguing."

"Good." Awash with relief, Jacques flicked the reins and pushed Midas a bit faster for the final mile.

***A Lady's Past* is available now.**

Also by A.S. Fenichel

HISTORICAL ROMANCE

The Wallflowers of West Lane Series

The Earl Not Taken

Misleading A Duke

Capturing the Earl

Not Even For A Duke

The Everton Domestic Society Series

A Lady's Honor

A Lady's Escape

A Lady's Virtue

A Lady's Doubt

A Lady's Past

The Forever Brides Series

Tainted Bride

Foolish Bride

Desperate Bride

Single Title Books

Wishing Game

Christmas Bliss

An Honorable Arrangement

HISTORICAL PARANORMAL ROMANCE

Witches of Windsor Series

Magic Touch

Magic Word

Pure Magic

The Demon Hunters Series

Ascension

Deception

Betrayal

Defiance

Vengeance

CONTEMPORARY PARANORMAL EROTIC ROMANCE

The Psychic Mates Series

Kane's Bounty

Joshua's Mistake

Training Rain

The End of Days Series

Mayan Afterglow

Mayan Craving

Mayan Inferno

End of Days Trilogy

CONTEMPORARY EROTIC ROMANCE

Single Title Books
Alaskan Exposure
Revving Up the Holidays

Visit A.S. Fenichel's website for a complete and up-to-date list of her books.

www.asfenichel.com

WRITING AS ANDIE FENICHEL
Dad Bod Handyman (Lane Family)
Carnival Lane (Lane Family)
Lane to Fame (Lane Family)
Changing Lanes (Lane Family)
Heavy Petting (Lane Family)
Summer Lane (Lane Family)
Hero's Lane (Lane Family)
Icing It (Lane Family)
Mountain Lane (Lane Family)
Christmas Lane (Lane Family)
Texas Lane (Lane Family)
Building Lane (Lane Family)
Dragon of My Dreams
Turnabout is Fairy Play
Soul of a Vampire (Brothers of Scrim Hall)
Soul of a Reaper (Brothers of Scrim Hall)
Soul of a Dragon (Brothers of Scrim Hall)

Soul of a Wolf (Brothers of Scrim Hall)
Soul of a Demon (Brothers of Scrim Hall)
Soul of a Phoenix (Brothers of Scrim Hall)

Visit Andie's website for the most up to date list.

www.andiefenichel.com

About the Author

A.S. Fenichel (Andie Fenichel) gave up a successful IT career in New York City to follow her husband to Texas and pursue her lifelong dream of being a professional writer. She's never looked back.

Andie adores writing stories filled with love, passion, desire, magic and maybe a little mayhem tossed in for good measure. Books have always been her perfect escape and she still relishes diving into one and staying up all night to finish a good story.

Originally from New York, she grew up in New Jersey, and now lives in Missouri with her real-life hero, her wonderful husband. When not reading or writing she enjoys cooking, travel, history, and puttering in her garden. On the side, she is a master cat wrangler and her fur babies keep her very busy.

www.asfenichel.com

facebook.com/a.s.fenichel
twitter.com/asfenichel
instagram.com/asfenichel
bookbub.com/authors/a-s-fenichel
tiktok.com/@asfenichel?
pinterest.com/asfenichel

I